Mayyar Hayel AlQahtani (Mila), CEO of the Metarix, was born in the Kingdom of Bahrain but is originally from Saudi Arabia. She is an artist, author, lyrical writer, producer, developer, and artificial intelligence creator. She is also the creator of the Artloids app.

To my family and my team that have always had faith in me.

To the kings and queens, gods and goddesses, princes and princesses of the century.

Mayyar AlQahtani (Mila)

20/20 VISION

AUSTIN MACAULEY PUBLISHERS™
LONDON • CAMBRIDGE • NEW YORK • SHARJAH

Copyright © Mayyar AlQahtani (Mila) 2022

The right of Mayyar AlQahtani (Mila) to be identified as author of this work has been asserted by the author in accordance with Federal Law No. (7) of UAE, Year 2002, Concerning Copyrights and Neighbouring Rights.

All rights reserved. No part of this publication may be reproduced, stored in a retrieval system, or transmitted in any form or by any means, electronic, mechanical, photocopying, recording, or otherwise, without the prior permission of the publishers.

Any person who commits any unauthorized act in relation to this publication may be liable to legal prosecution and civil claims for damages.

The age group that matches the content of the books has been classified according to the age classification system issued by the National Media Council.

ISBN – 9789948825982 – (Paperback)
ISBN – 9789948825999 – (E-Book)

Application Number: MC-10-01-4916638
Age Classification: E

Printer Name: iPrint Global Ltd
Printer Address: Witchford, England

First Published 2022
AUSTIN MACAULEY PUBLISHERS FZE
Sharjah Publishing City
P.O Box [519201]
Sharjah, UAE
www.austinmacauley.ae
+971 655 95 202

Drop the gun and follow the vision.

The power of being holistic tells you who you are in the stream of creation.

Aesthetic guide book of the century.

To the next generation and to the past, with acceleration.

To the kings and queens, gods and goddesses, princes and princesses of the century.

"Sunflower – I like that power – push me up to the tower – It's the final hour."

"You give me the gift of life of the mighty, meet up in an empty pool party, blowing up candy, skipping all the fight, white flicker peeps on this cloud, its rowdy."

"My skin self-regenerates, my body levitates, my mind it meditates, my flight is emirates."

Prologue

Optech is an optic, a clear 20/20 vision of intention and creations…aesthetic guide book of the century, founded by a low-key superhero. Half-motivational guide book, some fiction stories, of the past and future where vibranium is real and spaceships are above us, an abundance of wild.

If you believe, you will achieve. If you think it's too late, you already gave up…and if you give up, life gives up on you, then just when you think that there's no coming back. You just come back STRONGER.

A secret to dream fulfilment and the power of being holistic, finding where you are in the stream of creation. And uncovering what the universe has in hold for you by simple steps to get you through the loading process we call life.

Read: Between: The: Lines;

cout << "Some based in real-life. some based in dreams. Some implemented into reality" end

The 20/20 vision explained

Chapter 1
In My Blood

New Year's Eve of 2020 and only 30 minutes before midnight, I got lost in the middle of the Giza Pyramids desert in Egypt.
White horse, black dress, long wavy black hair, glowing fair skin, 23-year-old girl lost in the middle of the desert.
Wearing my Air Pods but missing my phone, I checked my pocket and only found my 'Crave' lipliner in my pocket…How did I end up lost? I mean, horse riding is my passion,
It's what I do, IT IS IN MY BLOOD….

IT IS IN
MY
BLOOD….

Hey, pretty little thing! I couldn't imagine a more promising way to deliver this message to you than through this book, I feel like I am a warrior princess that has spent pretty much all her life singing and painting and hoping for someday to be with my prince charming.

I spent a majority of my life wandering because I was stubborn and because I felt like I should chase after what I want, and that was really selfish and only led me to a lot of trouble and chaos and ups and downs. It's a way of universe trying to tell me that 'You will keep falling and mistakes will keep on repeating until you learn from them,' which is so true by the way. Until you learn to fix your mistakes…you will just keep on going on and on in that same loop over and over again….do you agree?

I woke up on the last day of 2019, one day to 2020. I usually love celebrations and holidays, I used to take them very seriously and loved to be a part of whatever the hottest event that's going on around, but something about being 23 feels different. I have had too much fun in the past doing so much amazing fun things and adventures that got me in A LOT OF TROUBLE. Yes, I had a glowing, golden, shimmery vibe all my life of happiness and had a habit of turning all my fantasies to realities, yes…or no… not a habit I would say…it was who I am, always gripping onto my glowing beam and always smelling like a combination of dream and butter-shea combined. I believed in YOLO before people started saying yolo. Because you really do only live once, once you believe in more lives, it gets complicated and you get stuck on the thought of 'will you be in the next life rather than focusing on your current life?' and that will just cause you a hell-ton of stress and anxiety and depression, which is why praying is so important, and I will explain that soon in a different chapter… So the last day of 2019 and finally the

year we all have been waiting for, 2020 is just a day away; a new beginning. Coming in HOT…
I decided to go do the thing I love the most for new years', and it's horse riding. I have a medieval look when I go horse riding, mainly because I generally love having a modern medieval dress on and love dresses in general. No, no, no, this isn't a chick book, that's just me…….but there's much to learn here, even for you boys out there. You and your shinny pistols. Life is what you make it, God just looks after you and listens to your prayer.

So I put on my black dress and I couldn't be happier that I was going horse riding on the night of new years', starting 2020 with a black cape on. All my friends were going too. They decided to meet me at the highest point of the desert, right next to the pyramids; so close, I could walk right inside of it. I picked up my white Arabian horse from the stable, left my phone with the guide and sprinted off like I was in a race. I thought that they would catch up but the music started disconnecting from my Air Pods and before I knew it, I was in the middle of nowhere. I can't even hear the breeze, just silence…So dark I can't see anything; just the shadow of the pyramid and the sky…oh how the sky speaks! It speaks in colours: green, platinum, dark navy blue, a bit of red, it spoke…the sky right above the pyramids spoke. Like there was some kind of open gates to heaven up there. It was just beautiful. I went off my horse and started gazing at the sky…just so precious…so welcoming…an invitation was coming…I could feel it. But what? Something so amazing I couldn't even know yet.

My horse heard a noise of a pack of over 15 horses running together. I could hear people screaming 'YA! YA!

YA!!! YAA!!!' And I could hear the sound of the horses' steps coming closer. It sounded like an army was coming my way…my horses ears went up…I knew he was on alert mode. And he froze…no, no, no, no, no! No! Just NO!

My horse ran off with the pack, leaving me stranded alone in the desert… I laughed. 'Such a good adventure! … but I don't want to miss the fireworks and it is probably going to start in 10 minutes! … Dear God… please help me get through this…'

Minutes later, a man with a horse comes close to me and he asked me if I needed help. Well, obviously I needed help. I'm stranded in the middle of the desert. He took me behind him on the horse and we took off. Less than a minute later, I witnessed the fireworks in the sky and right behind the pyramids, the colours were amazing. That and the sky and the whole combination of being rescued gave me goosebumps. Something was up, 2020 is coming in hard, like how a 1000cc motorbike would come in drifting on a corner with an extension on; 2020 wasn't joking, it was magical. Something is up and we will find out.

Anyways, the moment we entered the stables area, he got off the horse and walked the horse while I was on top of it. I thanked him a lot for his help. I don't know what would have happened to me if I was all alone there. At least I got to see the fireworks on my way back.

I found my horse back in the stable and I just sat there waiting for my friends around a bonfire, it was a bit chilly. I was a little upset that things didn't go the way that I wanted them to. But oh well, what an adventure.

From what I gathered in life, there are some basic things that happen, right in between 20–24 years of age. You have a very possible chance of going through a quarter-life crisis. It is a way of the universe trying to tell you to correct yourself if you have done wrong.

Some people go through it and think that they are not worthy of life and they can't correct it. They either decide to kill themselves by an overdose of a substance/combination of substances, or they can't take it and they end up fucking up even more.

No darling, you have to have faith

No darling, you have to be strong

No darling, you have to embrace it

No darling, you can't give in to it and give up

And once you hear that call, you have to listen to it and give in to it, and embrace it, don't give up.

Once you decide that it's too late anyways and there's no coming back, that's the moment where you give up. And if you give up, life gives up on you.

And if life gives up on you, you will give up not on the situation, but on yourself and if you give up on yourself,

You're lost.

Chapter 2
Holistic

Note: * Get a personal journal book. * This helps you accelerate and elevate to a better version life path.

Growing up, I was inspired by writers so I always kept my diary close to me and always wrote down how I felt. And every night I would answer these selected questions:
Write down 5 things you were grateful for today:

Write down how you connected with your higher power today:

Did you upset anyone? Write down who. Did you help anyone? Write down who and why?

I love to better understand myself because you always need to understand what you want to have control over. For example, do you want to break the law? Study law and become a lawyer. In order to break the rules, you have to learn them.

Another example, do you love hacking? And want to hack? Well I advise you study cyber-security and learn how the system works to be able to exploit it.

It's not so similar to your life, but to have control over anything good or bad, you need to study it and learn it. Movie producers always inspired me. Movies inspired me so much that whenever I start looking at a movie, I can't enjoy it so much. I get distracted with where the lightning is and where the crew is sitting and how the actor memorized his script and the way he is presenting it to the camera.

When I see paintings, I get distracted trying to understand where the shading started and ended, and how creative the artists was and what was he/she thinking about. I meditate. I meditate so much because I appreciate so much.

Oh, and because since I was little, I always told myself that I was an artist. And I believed it.

Holistic is being self-proclaimed, not officially, but self-proclaimed. And often it results in talents and gives you a vision of what you can be. And if you take it seriously, then that vision becomes a prediction of what you can be, and if you work hard to become it and really believe in it.

Now I don't mean believe in it like how you believe that Red bull will always be outside waiting for you…in the supermarket... just there waiting for you every day, so u can sleep good at night knowing that your Vimto or red bull will be waiting for you in the morning. NO. I mean having a BURNING DESIRE. THAT YOU BELIEVE IN IT SO MUCH YOU BELIEVE IN IT AS MUCH AS YOU WANT TO BREATH!

Yes, I believe as much as I want to breath that I am an artist; self-proclaimed. I don't doubt being one; I don't take opinions; but when I do, I get good feedback. But why don't you really want to take opinions...

Me: 'Hey Jasmine, do you like my song that I wrote today? Do you like it?'

Jasmine: 'OH MY GAWDDDDD, IT IS SOO GOOOOD'

Me: 'Hey Jasmine, do you like this painting I did?'
Jasmine: 'OH MY GAWWWD! That's SO PRETTTY!'

Me: 'Well... I don't know, I'm bit... eeeeh... well... Okay.'

Asking for opinions might flatter you too much even when you barely put any effort into it. You don't really want to ask for opinions, you want to believe. You CAN ask for opinions, but don't depend on them or take them too seriously. You're only good once you go big. GO BIG OR GO HOME!

Plus, taking opinions from the wrong people can really put you down, and we don't want that now do we?
We want to RISE. And implement our visions into reality.

If it's what you want to do, and if you BELIEVE in it as much as you want to breath, you need to have the burning passion and desire to proudly say: I AM AN ARTIST. I AM A FOOTBALL PLAYER. I AM A COMEDIAN. I AM AN ACTOR/ACTRESS. I am. I am. I am. I am. I am. I will be. I will be. I will be. I will be. I will be.
Keep it a secret between you and yourself if you please, but at some point in this book, you will have to build the courage to reveal yourself to the world. And that's when you get a MAJOR RUSH OF DOPAMINE. You will get SO HIGH on success, you will only want more. And more, the key to finally stop thirsting for success and desire, because I assure you, you will get addicted.

Once you become grateful for what you have.
So easy, yet so complicated? Not really complicated.
Very obvious…

Being Holistic makes you apart of the inter-connective fabric of reality.

The holistic life is about living your life, caring for it, balancing it and bringing health to all aspects of self and all major areas of life; always look at the bigger picture when you approach.

I got two eye sights, a pear that I see with 'the normal eyes' and one I also see with but in my mind, it's called:
VISUALIZING

For example:
An Architect can see blueprints of a building in their head, they can map it in their minds.
A chef; once they visualize the ingredients, they pour together.

Whenever I walk anywhere that is crowded, I visualize flying drones above me and I can see a blueprint of where I am. I can see the bigger picture.

It's like zooming out of a zoomed in picture.
Try zooming out of your life.

Once you see the bigger picture,
see where you fit in in life.

One assignment I did for my scientific thinking class, shout out to Professor/Doctor: Ghada – scientific thinking Professor:

Critical thinkers often always look for the best direct way to reach their goals and logically and precisely analyse them… WHY…?
Because they have a goal? Why…
Because they are motivated to do it.
That's how motivation is linked to critical thinking.

Understanding motivation can indeed help a person set their goals, and set their aim. Understand what's in the box and what's next to the box, understand themselves and live in the moment.

Appreciating the moment is everything.

We must learn to accept the things that we have no control over and learn to live a little. Learn to appreciate what we have, and hope for better things to come.

Once you free yourself and your mind, only then will you be able to free your soul; and once you free your soul by understanding that there are a few things that you can't change and learn to accept it, then you will be able to see better. Once you see better, you get better life vision. That's all about having the 20/20 vision.

To see through the light and love what you have.

– Mayyarih

Visualize yourself, visualizing yourself can unlock something called 'Precognition', which is the ability to see the future, before it happens. A vision.

It could unlock your full potential. And it will come, once it comes, you will know. You just have to BELIEVE.
Once you practice mindfulness by meditation, feel your breath, and take deep breaths. Keep yourself relaxed and stress-free.

Recognize and respect the powers of your body. Understand that each one of us is unique. If you are

Born, then you are chosen; and if you're chosen, then don't let this chance go. And if you purchased my book, then well, you definitely are chosen because I know that whoever is interested in this book is probably the next BIG BANG of the universe.

Eat clean foods, treat your body with respect.

Focus on positive relationships, keep your innocence with you; these are my friends, these are my family.
Yes, yes, yes, a lot of us are friendly, I understand. But with a population of 7 billion people and now because of Covid-19 we are decreasing, still… if someone's path in life doesn't at all benefit you in any way, let them go. Yes, yes, I know it's not fair… yes… but it kinda is. That's how life goes. If someone in this life DOES NOT BELONG IN YOUR LIFE, you guys don't have ANY hobbies in common or any sort of connection whatsoever, and having the same taste in music doesn't count,

Then just LET. THEM. GO.

Fate will unite you with your kind once you give in to the universe and become a part of the inter-connected fabric of reality.

Recycle energy.
Sleep well, your beauty sleep really matters and counts.

Let yourself grow.

Don't give up on practicing what you want to do, make time for yourself, and education is key. Once you give up on education because of anything… education doesn't only mean that you will have a great job; it means that you will exercise your mind more and have responsibilities and commitments and exercise your mind even more for exams that could potentially unlock A LOT of creativeness, and meet new people, and socializing with the community builds up your ambition to ask more from this life and to take the first step into fulfilment… Yes, that's kind of a cheat
code right there. I know I will be getting my masters after I graduate university as an artificial intelligent.

Love life, and be respectful.
Love love, love air, love the mirror, love your hair, love your skin, love sunflowers, love rose petals, love tiny baby cupids, love gaming, love glowing LED lights, love peace, love serenity, love harmony, love wisdom. Love knowledge, love passion, love elegance, love confidence, love science, love the moon, love space, love the iron man, love meals and food, love ice cream, love love, love Disney, love imagination, love creativity, love family, love people, love the world, love and peace.

Love and peace.
Love and peace.
Love and peace.
Love and peace.
Love and peace.
Love and peace.

Embrace who you are
Don't decide what you want, it will come once you

Connect.

Chapter 3
The Rat Race

If you are ever in a situation where you are in a RACE.

Be the turtle, work slowly towards your success, don't be the rabbit, because the rabbit was jumping and running so fast towards the finish line, with the ego very high, he lost at the end anyway.

Words psyche told me – Dr N,

Your limit, is THE UNIVERSE.

The sky isn't the limit.

YOUR LIMIT, IS THE UNIVERSE.

It's galactic.

You can have it all in your hands, right there. Go ahead, just do it. It's there.

Success and dream to reach there one day, daydreaming is envisioning, and that's your third eye right there. Anything bad you envision won't happen, so don't worry about it; that's just nonsense.

Your progress is all that counts.

Visions are seldom what they seem…
if you hear a wake-up call or see a vision,
throw your gun and chase it!

Chapter 4
Levitate

My body levitates, my mind it meditates, my skin self-regenerates.
It is important to understand your beliefs, your belief is who you are, and it shapes you. In order to set yourself free, and regain power and full control over your life, you need to understand your beliefs.
Do you hear a voice in your head? When you read… can you hear something in your head reading? Your voice maybe? Or a voice that you think that would match this story? Any voice? That you have control over in your head? Yes that, use that voice to talk and have conversations with yourself, talk to yourself in your head and ask and wonder…what are you really?
What do you believe in? Do you believe that a pink shirt will make you look ugly?
Do you believe that the world is round or flat?
Do you believe that one day you will become something amazing in life?
Do you believe that one day you will be famous?

Do you believe that in order to become famous, you have to rebel?
Do you believe that in order to keep one of your friends, you have to lie to the other friend?
What you believe turns into actions you will eventually do, and your beliefs and actions are statements of who you are from within.
Your actions and beliefs define you. They define who you are as a person.

Understand your beliefs, and reshape them if they need correcting.

Chapter 5
The Heavens Have Ears

Person 1:
Prayed for: POWER – LOVE – MONEY

Person 2:
Prayed for: PEACE – JOY – LOVE

Person 3:
Prayed for: KNOWLEDGE – GRACE – BEAUTY

Person 4:
Prayed for: PROTECTION and SUCCESS

Each prayer that you see in the examples above, are prayers that define the person's priority in life.
Four very different personalities.

Person one, prayed for power – love and money.

This person likes to be in charge; this person is an all or nothing kind of person; this person has empathy and desire for love, but might do anything to get the power and the money. Two very strong elements: power and money. And one drug: love. That's so toxic it could lift you so high or drag you down. Love would probably be this person's karma if he committed any wrongdoings.

Person two prayed for Peace – Joy – Love.
This person desires to escape the reality that we live in, away, to fulfil their life with good vibes. Now this person attracts good-vibed people by nature. Yes, BY NATURE. What you hope for and wish for, what you fill your mind with, is your reality. Like a saying in Arabic: انه االعمال بالنيات
If you hope for peace – joy – and love, you will find yourself surrounded by nature, with good vibes.

Person three prayed for knowledge – grace – beauty. Now this person likes shooting up to the skies, wants to find a cure for something, wants to hang trophies and certificates on their wall. This person wants knowledge, wants wisdom and information, and still maintain beauty and grace. This person will dive to self-care, and will be attracted to other smart people by nature.

Person four prayed for protection, for themselves and their family. This is a family person. Maybe their family is there and there's too much care in their hearts towards them, or maybe they are…but maybe they are not. Either way, this person is serene with themselves.

Whatever you HOPE for and WISH for, will happen. Just HOPE FOR THE BEST.
Your intentions deep down are the reality of who you are.

Prayer guides you to where you want to be. The moment you want to be in
(if you imagine it and see it happen… it will happen); all you need is imagination – determination – prayer. All your dreams will come true.

Listen to me young souls. If I say something, I mean it. A burning desire is what you need. To really, deeply want something to happen…so, so bad.
As much as you want to breath.

That determination will lead you to success and that's the KEY. **DETERMINATION.**
COMMITMENT
INSIST on it happening.
KEEP PUSHING.
Fight for what you love.
Reach and do what you want and please.

If you don't have HOPE,
then start having HOPE.
Shoot for the moon, you might land among the Stars.

Exercise:
Everyday write one thing that you saw HOPE in:

I saw hope today in_____My father's eyes, when he got the call that he got promoted_.

Everyday, write one thing that gave you FAITH.

Today I saw faith in_____the sunset, and how the colours in the sky were changing_____.

If you don't take a moment to:
Appreciate
Meditate
Build HOPE
Build FATH
Clear your intentions
Build a healthy diet
Build a healthy lifestyle

Build healthy relationships and cut off bad relationships;
Then, just pray to be saved.
Because that's what you will be needing.
To be saved. I had help, but I had to save myself.

^*+={*}^{]+=

Stop
Complaining,
Start
Praying,
Stop
Playing,

*Start
Praying.*

Chapter 6
Déjà vu

December 2019 – February 2020:

Something about the streets in Egypt kept making me feel
Déjà vu. The whole time. Like I'm sure either:
1 – I'm in a dream.
2 – I have seen this in a dream before.
3 – I AM SURE something paranormal is happening here.
Those 3 possible happenings, were happening.
With pretty much everything I was doing.

The universe either was trying to tell me that it's no big deal,
I'm safe, or it was telling me that I've had a past life as
an Egyptian goddess of some sort? No, no, no, no… none of
that.
It was just trying to prepare me for the journey, entering a
new phase in a new place, alone but angels, all around…
there were a lot of angels.
It was just the beginning; my angels wanted to make me feel
safe and the universe was telling me that I'm, for sure,

one hundred percent on the right path of life.

That made me feel safe.

At night I like to sit in the desert, or up on a hill, to watch satellites launch up to the sky. If I'm alone, I bring my Air Pods; if I'm with friends, I'd get my speaker and play loud Travis Scott music and stargaze. Meditation is a blessing, but overconcentration causes health issues; relax.

That and my countless wishes I make when I see shooting stars. This one time, I saw 3 shooting stars right behind each other, kinda like a chase. It was beautiful.

Learning the language of the skies means learning astronomy. Do you want to know the difference between a star and a satellite? Look at the sky. The one very close to the surface is most likely a satellite, and the others in the background are most likely stars… telescope is in my list. I really need me a telescope.

At that moment of meditation, something hit me.

We Only Live Once.

Chapter 7
It Looked Me in the Eyes

Clearing your debts and avoiding BAD ACTIONS:

First your need to clear your debts, financially *if any* and spiritually, if you have done someone wrong. Ask for forgiveness; if you don't want to, then do it between you and yourself, preferably at night time…before you go to sleep:

Say: *the name of the person you have done wrong* followed by, 'I'm sorry, please forgive me.'

But if you can correct it, please do. Clear yourself from all debts and problems.

That will help cleanse your spirit and you will enter the next level, and guess what's the next level?

CONSEQUENCE

And they are real. Very real.
For every action you make, something affects you.

If you find yourself in one of these situations because of certain life habits:

1 – The nature goes against you. The UNFORTUNATE or ZERO-LUCK, UNLUCKY stage might occur.

2 – Failure – Examination failure.

3 – Or like Regina Gorge, get hit by a bus.

4 – Losing money, losing items.

5 – Losing hope and faith, and change in some personality habits or attitudes.

6 – Physical pain, mental issues.

4 – Jailed or in a problem/situation.

5 – Dead.

Until stage 4, you still have THE WILL – THE DESIRE TO CHANGE, with a sprinkle of faith and hope in correcting your mistakes. God still is on your side and loves you.

Quit them now, and start over.

Living life, thinking that you can get away with anything, well there might be a lot of things you can get away with. You see, devils and demons, angels and gods are not only in the spirit life, and in heaven and hell, but that concept of

heaven and hell and angels and demons can also be applied in our world today. Did you know that hackers have an aura that glitches? When they walk next to electronics, they could make it glitch, and obtain control over it. Penetration testing and malware analysis is recommended but all these creatures live among of us.
Do you remember your mother, or someone that cares about you, once said:
Stay away from bad friends that give negativity.
Those are most likely, walking souls of the hell. On earth, yes, you are witnessing walking souls of hell right there. Not all of them, but some, yes; they exist.

Where do you fit in?
Are you an angel?
Are you the demon?
Or are you the devil?

I'm just human, means giving yourself an excuse to make a mistake.

We are prone to make mistakes.
We forget where we place our car keys, we forget to attend an appointment; some of us need the ability to write down a schedule and list down what we have to do, others needs a secretary to write down their appointments.
We sometimes tell a white lie.
We sometimes do the wrong thing in others eyes and get blamed for things we didn't do.
And it's all okay because it's a part of who we are,

The more we put ourselves in other people's shoes, the more we can understand. The more we let go of our stubborn mistakes, the more we start seeing things clearly.
Making a mistake doesn't mean that we are not worthy or that we are not enough.
Making a mistake doesn't make us the demons or devils.
It takes a lot to do the wrong thing over and over and over again and one wrong from another wrong is different.
Doing something wrong doesn't mean that you are a bad person. It's okay, we are just humans in the end. And we don't say it as an excuse.

We say it because it is a fact.

But taking advantage of the statement that we are humans to make mistakes is wrong.
You choose what defines you. We all choose; we all have the power to be who we want to be.
I am my mother's and father's daughter.
My mother is a goddess and my father is a pure-blooded Arabic angel and his blood screams royalty. No, he doesn't own a Mercedes, but his soul screams rich-pure-angel.

Sent to help other people.

How you feel about the people around you and how you feel about yourself really has an effect.
We are just human, but in other people's eyes; they see more than that; they can see purity, they can see good and evil, and what you do, defines you. Remember that.

If you go out and steal a car, then you are a thief. Being a thief by law doesn't mean that you are a bad person. It only means that you made the wrong choices.

It's never too late to change.

And when you think that it's too late and tell yourself that it's too late, that's when you already lost.
And if you give up on life, then life gives up on you.

This book is to show you the bigger picture; know who you are and where you fit in this life.

Because once you see clearly what you're doing wrong, only then can you change.

It all relates.

Ew, Junkies.

Woooooo, Knowledge elevates me.

Keep your hands clean.

Chapter 8
The Infinite Supplier

The supplier,

gifts, a lot of gifts, just like Santa.

Presents, a lot of presents, whatever you want.

Anything you want.

Pray.

Who to call for?

Your Higher Power.

But remember.
A Dream without a plan is just a WISH.

I Want it.
I Planned it.
I'm gonna get it and won't stop until I'm proud.

Chapter 9
Blame It On Me

'If you don't have something nice to say, don't say anything at all.'

If someone walks up to me and says:

'You hurt me in the past, you did this and that to me'.
It's my job to listen. It's not my job to talk back to them in a negative way; that will only result in:
1 – A misunderstanding.
2 – A fight.
3 – Angry souls, both you and them.
4 – Angels will get upset. They are not COMPLAINING.
Complaining is like:
Oh, the weather is so hot today! Oh, this jeans won't fit anymore!
They are not trying to criticize you, either.
They are simply trying to hear the words:

'I'm sorry, I didn't mean to, forgive me.'

And there's nothing wrong with being kind and apologizing.
Doing good brings GOOD KARMA and doing bad, brings
BAD KARMA. And you don't want BAD KARMA
in your life if you expect to live a healthy peaceful life.

Clear your debts that are bothering you. Let go of your past.
Live in today.
And;

Daily homework:
Whom did I hurt today?

Whom were you kind to today?

How did you show kindness?

No excuses.

Put the blame on yourself.

Even if you don't see it.

Put yourself in their shoes.
Even if you cant.

Put the blame on you.
And if you can't,

then your stubborn negative soul needs to be saved.
Pray for forgiveness. Until you see the light at the end of the
tunnel. Look, I'm not trying to turn you into a bad person.

I'm trying to turn you into a good person. I'm trying to free you; I'm trying to give you a taste of the honey glazed donut with 2 scoops of ice cream that I had in life.

And never say that this life isn't meant for you. If you're born, then you are CHOSEN.

Chapter 10
Pulse

It is very important to maintain healthy relationships. Good angels that walk among us should stay in your life unless you end up getting more responsibilities, like job – marriage – kids come along. Then, only then, if some obstacles come by you, and you sit in a point where you have to make a choice, choose LOVE and FAMILY and WORK over anything. That is the main foundation of our existence: to love and to know. 'Know' comes from knowledge.

Set limits with people, draw down your boundaries, know your inner circle (YOU). Your surroundings, notice them (your FAMILY and loved ones).

Your purpose (work and workmates).

And your destiny (your hobbies and talents and your surroundings that support them or have a common interest in them).

There has to be a line in your life. This person is this. That person is that.

Declare and identify the people around you. With my family I will present:
respect, love, motivation, support, gratitude.
With my lover/soulmate I will present:
Honesty, loyalty, respect, love, support, gratitude, passion.
With my work I will present: ambition and discipline.
With my hobbies and talent I will present: passion and dedication.
With my friends, I will present: support, care.
Every group you line up that are around, you should present a certain kind of attitude towards them. Not because you are not authentic, you are authentic, but you are not playing around. You are here to achieve and you need to give yourself SPACE.

Cout << "Eye of dragon: Eye of love and wisdom"\n <<

Seeing you through the eye of Dragon.

Chapter 11
The List

Find your interest and passion,

and divide them into sections,

hobbies/self-care/education/work/surroundings

And give each section some time in a time table.

Writing down a schedule

Close this Book now and plan out your schedule List three priorities
And fit them in your life;
where you give them a chance to grow.

I deserve more.

Chapter 12
No One Can

Some things in life we can find out, other things we can work out.

But personal issues are a journey that you have to find out for yourself.

Layla: 'Do you have a plan for your next step in your career life?'
Lia: 'Yes, sure I do.'
Layla: 'What is it?'
Lia: 'I'm not sure yet…'
Layla: 'So you don't have a plan?'
Lia: 'Ummm…ah…ummmmm!'

Your life is a **journey**…only you could uncover your plan. I'm not here to help you find a plan; that's something only you can find for yourself. It's your mission to shape your plan
and set it up.

I only help prepare you for what's coming next.
You have to have a plan, but you have to be the one making your plan and no one else.

Create your journey, and trust it.

Chapter 13
Bad Luck

After a hurricane, comes a rainbow.

If you want the rainbow, you gotta put up with the rain.

Do good, get good.

Negative people have a problem for every solution. Take a break.

Stay away from people that constantly remind you of your mistakes.

You will see clearly then. And go over this book again.

Catch a flight, escape.

Chapter 14
Me, Mine, Moi

Stop letting people influence your decisions; after all… this is your life that you will live. This is your path. We all die in our graves alone someday; it's about you. And there is nothing wrong or selfish about that.

Being selfish is okay. But remember. Everything that goes over the top, shoots right back against you.

Doing too much of anything is bad, so we need to have a balance. No white, no black, look for the GREY. The balance in between.

My family and life expects me to do the basics: Finish my education,

Work,

Be independent.

That's it. Anything else that comes in the way is a choice, your choice to make, how you finish your education and work and be dependent is up to you. Your choice.

Have a choice, don't be forced.

I remember the story of the gunner in a supermarket. He stayed silent all his life and took problems from other

people; they treated him very bad and poorly. One day, he picked up a gun and shot everyone in the supermarket.
Silent but deadly.

Chapter 15
See My Crown

Waking up in the morning... I look at myself in the mirror. I feel like half the universe's beauty is right there. I don't care what people will say about that. I know I'm the BOMB. I don't care how people feel about that, on EARTH...I slay. Confidence is attractive, confidence means power and strength, confidence is smart, confidence is beautiful, confidence is wisdom, confidence is serene, confidence is kind, confidence is right, confidence is key, confidence is dignity, confidence is pride, confidence is hope.

Confidence is the foundation of success and achievements

Confidence is who you are.
When you love yourself and accept yourself fully, you show confidence.

The anxiety is lying to you, sweet-cheeks!

My attire, my dress… my face and my skin lullabies drift me away.
All the flowers would have very extra special powers. Being patient is a virtue
but it's hard to stay strong all the time.
When I stumble, I play music. When I see shadows, I sing.
When I feel down, I cry.
I wake up the next morning and brush my hair.
Run away with me.
Your name is constantly on my diary.
No one will love me more than myself.
I dress myself, and I take care of myself.
But I am on a journey.
And you make my journey easier.
Your eyes are so filled with pain, they hold you down. Your energy they drain, it makes you frown.
Your mind, they like to chain it makes you howl.
Seeking peace in day, they make you cowl Owl,
Owl.
Being up at night really effects your immune system. Get your beauty sleep.
Schedule a specific time you have to be home.
Schedule a specific time you get to sleep.
Wake up early.
All bosses that have a lust towards success wake up at 5 am.
Because it gives them more hours in the day, and just enough for coffee and a shower.
Hold on to your youth and never grow up.

Keep on dreaming.

Visualize your highest self. And start becoming it.

You're as beautiful as a rose.

Honey, your soul is golden.

You are important.

The million dreams are keeping me awake.

I get myself flowers.

I buy myself gifts.

The sun will rise and we will try again.

Self-love starts with acceptance.

You got this.

You are the hero of your own story.

Chapter 16
Lovers

If you have been
Let down
Broken
Hurt

By someone so special to you,

People are not the same.

Don't let someone toxic ruin your life, especially your love life. Once you feel that this person is:
SUPPORTING YOU
LOVING YOU
ALWAYS ON YOUR SIDE EVEN IF YOU ARE WRONG
CARING FOR YOU
RESPECTING YOU
LOYAL TO YOU
CRAVES YOU
GIGGLES AND BLUSHES

WISHES THE BEST FOR YOU
MOTIVATES YOU
KEEPS UP WITH YOU
SACRIFICES FOR YOU

Appreciate them, hold on tight to them, and never let them go.
Those are angels sent from above and made especially for you.

And once you meet them, you will know If it's not the time.
Someday it will be if it's meant to be, it's meant to be.

If it's not meant to be, then it never was yours.
People make mistakes, people change.
But anyone who wasn't what I mentioned in the previous page, and hurt you instead, don't give them time to change or fix their bad habits or mistakes, move on.
They are on a different timeline and path in life than you are.

Understand
Accept
Trust

You deserve what's enough for you.

Take your time to bloom but live in the moment.

It wasn't hard to fall for you.

Hey, sunshine! I need you.

I'm always tired, but never of you.

I choose you. And I'll choose you, over and over, without pause.

If you have love in your heart, let it show.

You are my heart in human form.

I'm hopelessly in love with you.

Your love lifts me higher and higher.

Your love keeps me safe.

Your love made me reach for the stars.

**One day we will sip on tea in San José,
Vienna, Paris, Amsterdam.**

And all over the world.

I love me, and I love you for loving me so much.

Chapter 17
Fear

A lot of mistakes had to occur for me to learn, a lot of things went bad and the wrong way, a lot of problems…
I felt like I was sinking… I want it all to end…
I want to fit in and be accepted; not by the world, but by myself, I just wanted peace.
Will I ever get it with all the mistakes I have made?
Will I ever get a chance to move on and start a new chapter?
Will my past ever come up?
We have all done or said things we are not proud of.
After releasing this book, how many people will talk about me?
I am sorry if I have done anyone wrong. I didn't mean it.
After releasing this book, will I get criticized?
Will I get criticized by people that know for a fact that I am a good person, but they just own a big mouth?
Despite my confidence in myself, fear is in all of us.

Killing fear without killing empathy is a mission.

But possible.
Very possible.

If you ever lied, and you were afraid of the lie, pray for forgiveness,
1 – State the name of your God 2 – Mention your sin
3 – Mention cause and reason of your sin 4 – Ask for mercy and forgiveness.

'Forgive me for I have lied. I wish there were other ways for me to have control over the situation. Unfortunately, it had to result in a lie, and it was only to maintain the situation I was in, and it was only to prevent trouble and problems that the truth would have caused.
Forgive me and have mercy on me. I am sorry.'
Remember that for every action has a reaction, prayers can save you and get you out of it. Prayers, and for sure, your prayers will be heard.
Remember that the moment that you forgive yourself and the moment that you accept yourself and vow to forget and let go,

Negativity lets go of you.

If fear gets in your head,
Find the source of the fear, understand what's triggering fear from within you.
Once you know the cause of your fear, you will be able to face it, deal with it and overcome it.

Every fear you face has its own time for you to face it. Don't rush it, it will come.

Everything has its time for you to deal with it. Some fear you can deal with right now.

Other fears you can deal with tomorrow.

More fears you can deal with next month or year.

Every fear has its time and schedule of when you will face it and

keep that in mind.

Note to readers: Sarcasm, take it seriously.

Thinking will not overcome fear, but action will.

Fear does not stop death, it stops life.

The future belongs to freedom, not fear.

What we fear doing most is usually what we most need to do.

Fear is nothing more than a state of mind.

Being brave isn't the absence of fear; being brave is having that fear but finding a way through it.

Face your fears, have a conversation with fear, look it in the eyes, and then keep fear on your KOS list.
#KillOnSight

Everything beautiful is on the other side of fear.

Facing fear is a part of clearing your debts. Once you face your fear, and clear that debt,
you can move on.
Conquer it to thrive.

They won't know unless you TELL THEM. Actions speak louder than words.

Chapter 18
20/20

What is a 20/20 vision?
What is the 20/20 vision?
And who has it?

KNOWING WHAT YOU WANT

USING CREATIVITY

SENDING A MESSAGE

CANDIDATE FOR SOMETHING

LIFE IS WAITING ON

MAPPING YOUR VISION

FATE DIRECTS YOU

CONNECTING WITH PEOPLE

MAPPING IT ALL DOWN

LIST YOUR NEEDS

GET YOUR NEEDS

SEE IT HAPPEN

GETTING PREPARED

STAGE ONE PLAN A

STAGE TWO PLAN B

STAGE THREE PLAN C

CLIMBING THE TOWER

Climbing the tower takes time. IT'S OKAY! You will get there, keep on pushing,

MORE PREPARATION

Everything takes time, make sure it's perfect and exactly what you want. You got this, it's now or never. Set up a deadline, 5 years/10 years, some people get there in the same day; some people just when they lose hope, a miracle happens. This book is for believers. If you believe, you know
you will achieve no matter what.

MAKING IT HAPPEN

NO EXCUSES

NO FEAR

IMPULSIVITY

SLOW DOWN AND REWIND

DEEP BREATHS AND PRAY

CONFIDENCE

HOPE AND TRUST

SHOOT FOR THE STARS

AND BEFORE YOU KNOW IT

WINNING THE RACE FROM SPACE

Watching the whole world in nano

A Dream without a plan is just a wish.

Some people can do 3 things or 4 at once.

I planned it in silence.

They won't know unless you tell them.

Cout << "EXECUTION" <<

Show them

Amaze them

Wooo them

Make them go WOOOOOWWWW!

Put 1000 red lines under this one...

Walked in confidence Did it in silence
and SHOCK them

Note ** Unity is also a key fragment ** Whatever happened, happened. It is a part of your destiny, but now everything changes, so keep your scoop locked up tight and chase your dreams.